A modern story of a B.A.G
(British Asian Girl)

TINA
'N'
NIKIL

One
Sided-Love

Best Wishes
Rashmita
27-7-07.

A modern story of a B.A.G
(British Asian Girl)

TINA
'N'
NIKIL

One
Sided-Love

Rashmita Patel

DTF Publishers & Distributors
117 Soho Road, Handsworth
Birmingham B21 9ST

Published by
DTF Publishers & Distributors
117 Soho Road, Handsworth
Birmingham B21 9ST
U K
Phone: 0121 515 1183/551 7898
Fax: 0121 554 2676
e-mail:info@dtfbooks.com
website:www.dtfbooks.com

ISBN 1-901363-61-9
First published 2006
©2006, Patel, Rashmita

ACKNOWLEDGEMENTS

Dedicated to my beloved father:
Kalyanji S Patel
The memory of you will always be with us

A big thank you to my mother, for her encouragement and
support throughout the time

Especially to my loving husband Paresh, and my beautiful
son Vivek, for their enthusiasm and patience.

Many thanks to Nagina who has helped me along the way

With warm thanks to Ultimate Proof Publishing Services,
Cheltenham for their superb guidance and editorial skills.

To all those who have read and contributed to the
manuscript along the way.

'Mein mar java! You should have seen him! . . .'
As he sat there in his white shirt I
could see the outline of his body.
Man was he fit or what?

Tina is a B.A.G. (British Asian Girl) born and bred in Birmingham (UK) but finds herself trapped in a traditional Indian Culture

'N'

Nikil is a westernized young guy, who tries to please his parents but destroys everything for what he believes is love

1 Hi, I'm Tina Sinhasi. I'm Asian, as you may have guessed by my name. I'm 5 foot 5 inches tall; a good height for an Asian girl, wouldn't you say? I have dark-brown eyes and shoulder-length hair. I don't think it's important for you to know what religion I am. I mean, I hate everybody kicking up a big fuss about what I believe in and, anyway, it's a complicated issue all this religion stuff. I do sometimes wonder why everybody didn't just have one religion and then at least we wouldn't have so many problems as we do today.

I've got a degree in psychology, which, of course was different to what my parents expected me to study; it had to be either medicine or business. Forget that. I wanted to be a social worker. Nothing wrong with that, it was what I was interested in. Let me get back on track. This is a story about me and it's damn good. You know why, because it's the first time someone's going to tell you openly about what life's like here for us, the British Asian Girls or, as I say, B.A.Gs.

When did you last hear a story about an Asian girl having problems? I feel we Asian girls are brainwashed to a certain extent and always get told by our parents to stay away from guys. Now, how is that possible? Come off it! Be serious! How can you get through a day without mingling with guys? OK, to a certain point parents are right but come on, we're living in the 21st century, and things should change with time, shouldn't they?

The thing with us B.A.Gs is that nobody gossips when you're a kid but once you've passed puberty, everyone starts to think you're going to run off with the first boy you see. That's how it seems to them. It's damn complicated and it's even worse when a relative sees you in town having a conversation with a guy. That really gets them going!

'Your daughter was seen in town with a guy!'

One time I was in town and I saw Carlos from uni. He asked me if I had seen Lewis and Dan. I said I hadn't. Just then my auntie, Dimple, was passing by with her daughter and you should have seen her face. Instead of saying hello she just stood and stared, her eyes nearly popped out of their sockets!

Aunt Dimple was not my real aunt. I just called her auntie as a sign of respect. Anybody who was close to mum and dad were automatically classed as uncle or aunt, don't ask me why. I didn't like Aunt Dimple. She didn't live very far from us; in fact she lived right opposite, which made it worse because she could watch me all the time. She didn't work and spent most of her time indoors, cooking, cleaning and doing chores. She had one serious mouth on her; I called her Aunt Dimple, News Reporter because she always had something to gossip about.

When I got home my mum just leapt at me, and then the lectures started.

'I heard you were in town with an African boy? What were you doing with him?' and all that rubbish. Can you believe it? It was just an innocent conversation, which that stupid woman had screwed up and made into a kulfi. But hey, that's what it's like in our community. I can understand that people will talk. Our neighbours, even our relatives, will gossip. That's normal, but it's so damn irritating? I mean, if you don't talk to guys, how the hell are you going to socialize with them?

My best friend's mum was just as obsessed as mine. One time Rani bought some new clothes and her mum just hated the sight of them. Rani was so scared of wearing them or being seen in them. But, the thing is, they weren't as bad as she thought. Actually, I thought they were quite cool. They weren't mini skirts or anything revealing like that, it was the style she hated. 'Oh these are nice, Tina,' mum would say after dragging me into some fogey clothes shop and, of course, I had to say, 'Yes Mum, it's nice,' just so that I didn't hurt her feelings. But when she wanted to buy it, I'd look for the nearest exit! The problem is that our choice of clothes just wasn't the same. I always said to my mates that I thought it was an age problem. My parents just liked to make sure every part of me was covered, from head to toe. Ok, I could understand that they were looking after my welfare but come on, so what if a bit of my leg or arm was showing, it wasn't as though I was going out in my underwear was it? Well, as I was saying about Rani, her mum made such an issue of it that she decided to give all the new clothes away. Can't a girl keep up with fashion? Can you imagine if you went out wearing something from the 70s?

Another irritation was my uncle, Nil. Uncle Nil is dad's best mate so, as with Aunt Dimple, he was not my real uncle. He was another judgmental character. He came over every Friday to see dad and I'd often sneak into the house just to avoid him. If he saw me then I could count on it that he would have something to criticise me for, because that's how he was. He just hated it when he saw me talking on my mobile. He'd say,

'Tina, who are you talking to? I'm not stupid. I know it's a guy?'

Where did he get that from? Then my dad would give me this awful look and I'd have to hang up.

It was all down to conflicting pressures. I had to try and mix with everyone in the class but it was hard when I was expected to avoid the guys. Can you imagine going to class trying to ignore all the male pupils? I remember when we used to have drama at school and the teacher, Mr. Constable, put us in small, mixed sex groups to do a role-play. So, what do you do? Do you pretend they're not there or say to the teacher,

'Oh, I can't mix with the guys because my parents won't let me'.

Then there was Mrs. Tilley who always made us sit boy-girl so that we didn't talk and I was probably the quietest person in the room! But that's how it was and I'd walk around school trying to be the good darling my parents expected me to be.

All too soon I reached the age when the guys start

noticing me, and my parents start to get all fidgety about it. Then one day, they dropped a bombshell on me — marriage! At first it sounded foreign because my brain hadn't registered the word properly and then, when it sank in, I felt all feminine inside. To make matters worse, they add another word, 'arranged'. What did you say? I mean, I heard what they've said but I was trying to make sure I heard it right.

'I said, arranged marriage!'

'Arranged marriage! Are you serious mum?'

Then the lectures start coming thick and fast, about how wonderful arranged marriages are. OK, so everyone, according to parents, had an arranged marriage but that's how it was in their day. I mean, we were in the UK and our upbringing was different to theirs, wasn't it?

I don't know whether it's because of our strict culture but us B.A.Gs find it really hard to talk to our parents about relationships. I'm an only child. Sometimes it was great but it did have its disadvantages, especially when I wanted to talk to someone about boys. I couldn't really talk to mum and dad; it wasn't their kind of talk. Other relatives lived too far away to be much help.

I guess I was lucky because my dad isn't dead strict, not like the ones you'd hear about who locked their daughters away. My dad is quite relaxed, to a certain extent. He's a bus driver, he works irregular hours and I could never keep up with his shifts. OK, from time-to-time he has his moments but he isn't a bad dad. He was strict about me going out but then who could blame him? I mean his sister ran off with a Punjabi and I don't think dad took the news too well. He always told me that he didn't want me to turn out like Aunt Bindi.

One of the things about my dad I find hard to understand is that he isn't easy to talk to about issues, which my mates talked to their dads about, you know like further education, going away to study, marriage and that kind of stuff. As long as I wasn't in any trouble, he was happy.

Mum, on the other hand, is quite the opposite. She has a rotten temper, but her heart is in the right place. I found it easier talking to mum if I wanted to go out. Arranged marriages can be so complicated, sometimes my friends would ask,

'Tina, what exactly is an arranged marriage?' and I would shrug and say something like,

'Well, it's when your parents show you a selection of guys and you have to choose the one you fancy,'

But, hey, if they say you have to marry a particular guy then that's not arranged; that's what I would call a forced marriage. What I didn't understand was how the hell I was supposed to know if I loved the guy? I didn't think that just by looking at him I was going to fall madly in love with him. So, how did that bit happen? I supposed I'd just have to wait and find out. As my mum always said,

'It will come naturally; just wait and see.'

When mum mentioned an arranged marriage I was so shocked that I didn't know what to say but, funnily enough, they believed that as soon as they'd mentioned an arranged marriage I'd go along with it. Then they were on a mission to find what they considered to be the right guy for me. The relatives and neighbours were asked to look around for someone suitable for Tina. It all sounded so desperate. There would be at least one phone call a week saying a boy had been found for me.

Deep down, I knew I wasn't ready for marriage.

I was 22 and in my final year at uni. It wasn't easy handing in all those essays and it didn't help that I'd have to listen to my parents telling me that they had more guys for me to see. Wonderful, just wonderful! Don't get me wrong, I love my parents to bits but I just didn't like the way it was all handled. It was hard enough trying to fit in with my white friends without my parents hassling me about an arranged marriage, it all seemed too much. To tell the truth, I wasn't thinking of marrying until I was about 25. I just wanted to finish my studies, get a good job and enjoy a bit of life before getting tied down and having babies. I hadn't even given marriage a thought.

When I told my friends Sarah and Denise about this they found it extremely funny. It was OK for them; they could choose whom they wanted to be with. I wished I had that freedom of choice. I wanted my love life to be special, just like in some of those Bollywood films. I knew it was all a fantasy but I couldn't help dreaming. My ideal man would be someone like the actor, Shahrukh Khan: the body, brains and looks all wrapped into one. But where would I find someone like that? It's said that there's someone for everyone, I just wanted to wait and see if I would meet my special someone.

2   So, this is where the drama really started. They arranged for me to see a guy. Well, OK, maybe it was a bit exciting at first but I was a bit nervous. I mean, what would I say? 'Hi, I've come to check you out to see if you're Mr. Right?' We all went to my uncle's because that's where we decided to meet him. I didn't go over the top with my outfit and dressed in a beautiful shaded pink choli suit. Asian parents like to see their daughters dress traditionally: not in jeans and a t-shirt.

When the family arrived it took me at least twenty minutes to figure out which one I was supposed to be interested in marrying! There was the mum and dad and two guys, both about the same age. I didn't know who I supposed to look at! They were both smartly dressed and both looking at me, it was so embarrassing! I elbowed my mum and whispered in her ear,

'Who's the boy?'

She just looked at me.

'Tina, stop being silly, can't you see it's the one with the moustache? The other is his brother-in-law.'

Well it wasn't my fault they both looked the same

age! They could have shown me a photo beforehand instead of presuming I would know.

I spent the next few minutes discreetly glancing in his direction. I noticed he was doing the same as our eyes met a couple of times. So, OK, he wasn't that bad looking. He had a longish shaped face and a small moustache. His hair was very short and the front was spiked with a bit of gel. He was tall, fairly dark but cute and was smartly dressed in a beige suit. I wasn't exactly overwhelmed though I secretly gave him seven out of ten.

When my auntie finally took us out of the room, I got even more nervous. For the next half an hour we talked. This was the part I had been dreading but it wasn't half as bad as I thought. He was nice enough but when I started asking him about his career, man, you should have seen him, he wouldn't shut up! You won't believe what he did for a living. Yeah, he was a doctor; no wonder my parents liked him so much! When I asked him how much spare time he had, he said,

'None, of course! I'm a doctor!'

Typical. I quickly realised that there was no chance with this one. So, what if he earned a lot, I wasn't interested in that. He was a complete egotist and when he asked me what I did for a living, and I said I was studying to be a social worker, he turned his nose up. He talked as though it wasn't a qualified job and said he was looking for someone who had a similar career to his.

When I got home my parents wanted to know how it went. Well, it was nice that they asked me I suppose. I told them he wasn't the right guy and they were really disappointed. It was as if I'd really let them down.

'Tina, it's a good family,' said dad.

'Dad, he's not my type.'

Dad became impatient,

'You need to really think. You can't just say he's not your type!'

'Dad, I don't care if he's a doctor!'

'The whole family's educated and well settled,' argued dad.

I walked out at that point.

Sometimes I wondered whether they really did care about me, or whether they were just trying to get rid of me at the earliest opportunity. They didn't want to hear me say no, because he was a doctor. What was it with doctors? I mean why do parents think that money is the most important issue when marrying a daughter off? Why do they think that a guy has to be loaded to look after you? I would only say yes when I knew I was in love.

For a while I didn't see any more guys. I thought my parents had given up, but then mum arranged for me to see another guy at a wedding. By this time I had a bit of experience, and felt much happier about seeing another guy. This time I had questions ready to ask.

Again, I dressed up in a traditional Asian outfit. I don't know how they expected me to find time to talk to him but I went along with mum and dad. I was shocked to see it all packed out. I didn't go to weddings very often, I always stayed at home while my parents went.

We sat down by one of my aunties. The music was great: none of the traditional wedding songs but

modern Hindi songs. Luckily, I met my friend Deepa
there and we sat and talked for ages about arranged
marriages.

Deepa was a year older than me, and her parents
had already fixed her up with a guy called Krish. I'd
seen his photo; he looked very nice and was good
looking. Apparently, Deepa and Krish got on like a
house on fire and had quiet a lot in common. I felt a bit
envious of her because she had found everything she
wanted in a guy, looks, personality, and the brains of
course. I told her I had come to see a guy. She thought
it was all ace, I was so glad Deepa was there with me.
At least I would have her opinion too and I could always
count on Deepa to tell me the truth.

Mum came over and pointed to a guy who stood at
the back of the room with two other guys. Luckily, this
time I could tell which one she was pointing at. When I
showed Deepa the guy she made her feelings very clear!

'Sorry, Tina, no offence, but he is yuck!' I just looked
at her.

She was right, he was definitely not my type. Mum
asked if I liked him but he was too short and too chubby
for me. When I told mum, she actually agreed with me!
So that was that.

I think she knew that I was going to say no to this
one; thank goodness I wasn't asked to speak to him. I
relaxed after that and enjoyed the wedding with Deepa.
I could hear mum in the background talking to all my
relations about finding me a guy. It was quite
embarrassing, especially when they started looking me
up and down. I felt like everyone was examining me.
This was why I hated weddings because you could

suddenly become the centre of attention. Some may say that weddings are the best places to fix up couples but not on this occasion!

3   Out of the blue my grandad phoned from
     India. The line wasn't very clear but my
     dad managed to make out what he was
saying, then I heard other stuff like plane details and
flight numbers. I realized that my grandparents were
coming over. Well, this would be interesting. Maybe
my parents would get off my case while they were busy
making preparations for my grandparent's arrival. I was
really happy they were coming. It was going to be great,
as I knew they'd be bringing presents!

A few days later we went to pick them up from the
airport. As usual it wasn't just us, my uncles, aunts and
their families came too. It was a good job dad had hired
a minibus! It was my first trip to Heathrow and it was
really cool. While everyone waited in the coffee area I
checked out the planes. I loved watching them taking
off and coming in to land.

This was my grandparent's first visit to the UK. I had
only ever seen them in photos. I was quite looking
forward to meeting them. After a long wait, my dad
noticed my grandparents coming through arrivals, and
suddenly he went haywire, waving his hands about

madly. It was quite embarrassing. I thought he was
going to hit an old woman who was standing in front
of him! She had to move quickly to avoid being hit!
Then he started shouting loudly,

'Mama! Papa!'

I had to say something,

'Dad, shh!' I hissed.

Ignoring me he headed for the front entrance where
the passengers were coming out. It was chaos with big
hugs and greetings, and then my grandparents saw me.
I did my Asian greetings to Grandmum who then
grabbed me and cried out,

'Meri beti!' Which means 'my daughter'.

My grandparents chatted about their trip all the way
home. Grandad was really funny, I loved his sense of
humour. When we got home we all helped unload the
suitcases from the minibus before we sat down to eat.
Mum had cooked all her favourite dishes, chicken
samosas, onion bhaji and a delicious chicken curry.

After dinner my grandparents started to unpack their
suitcases. Mum wanted them to rest, as they looked
worn out. However, Grandmum was much more
interested in giving us the presents she had brought
from India. I have to say I was shocked to see what
looked like hundreds of poppadoms and pots of pickles,
which had leaked! They gave me some beautiful Asian
suits. It was a good job that the pickles hadn't leaked
onto them. Dad was really pleased when Grandad
handed him a stack of Bollywood films; Dad loved his
Bollywood film collection. They also brought mum
some lovely silk saris.

Later that evening we sat in the living room. Mum

and dad chatted to my grandparents while I watched TV. In the background I heard them talking about something to do with men. Grandmum had brought photos of some guys from India. I stared straight at the TV making sure they didn't know that I'd heard them. It was obvious mum and dad had spoken to Grandmum about my marriage. I heard mum whisper,

'I'll show them to Tina later.'

I was horrified! What's going on! Did they want me to go to India to get married? Then dad and Grandad left the room, leaving me alone with mum and Grandmum. I thought I'd make a dash for my room, but it was too late.

'Tina, can you come here please?'

I almost whispered in reply, 'What is it mum?'

'We want to show you something.'

Oh boy, I was in trouble! I went over and sat down. They didn't waste any time, Grandmum handed me the envelope.

'Take a look,' said mum,

I opened the envelope and took out the photos.

'What's this, mum?'

I wasn't sure what they wanted me to say. They both just looked at me.

'Who are they?'

I mean, it was obvious who they were but I pretended I had no idea.

'Your Grandmum brought these photos to see if you liked any of these boys for marriage.'

I could feel my blood boiling, it felt as if I was about to explode.

'No! I'm not interested!' I shouted and stormed out

slamming the door behind me.

I didn't care what they thought. I mean, they didn't waste much time! One minute I was looking at guys here and now India! Come off it! Were they *that* desperate to marry me off? What was the rush, I was their only daughter? I hadn't even thought about a guy from India. I mean, just imagine the problems we would have with even the basic stuff like language; clothes, music, everything!

I lay on my bed and tried to stop myself from crying but couldn't. Soon my pillow was wet and stained with my smudged eyeliner. I was so angry, I felt I wasn't wanted anymore. My grandparents seemed to have dug an even deeper hole for me. How was I going to get out of this? After an hour or so I heard mum call up the stairs.

'Tina can you come down and help me with the chapattis?'

I wiped my tears away and sat up. I felt a bit rude ignoring Grandmum, so I went downstairs. She was sat at the dining table and looked up at me as I walked past to get to the kitchen. I started to roll the chapattis and pretended nothing had happened. Luckily they didn't mention the photos, which was a relief because I couldn't face another row. To me it was all a farce.

For the next few days Grandmum gave me the cold shoulder. I tried to be nice to her but all I ever heard her say to mum was,

'I just want to see one family wedding before I die.'

So, she'd resorted to emotional blackmail. If she died before I got married was I supposed to feel guilty or something? This wasn't fair! I just wasn't interested in getting married, arranged or not, couldn't they see that?

The excitement I felt at having my grandparents around disappeared, and I started to wonder when they would leave, but it was just my luck that dad had invited them to stay longer. I had a feeling that until I got married none of them would be off my case.

For a while there was no mention of me seeing any new guys. I certainly wasn't going to bring it up, and I thought that if I did find a guy on my own, I would just be upfront and tell them. The only problem was that there wasn't anybody at uni who I really fancied. OK, so from time to time I had the odd crush, like I did with Ziggy, but it wasn't as though there was ever any real chemistry.

Then one day Aunt Sim and Uncle Jav arrived from London. I was so glad to see them!

I really liked my Aunt Simrin. She was like me, down to earth and I knew I could talk to her if I had a problem. Why hadn't I thought of her earlier? I could have told her about mum and dad trying to arrange my marriage.

I was relieved when Aunt Sim said they were staying for a while. After a few days I plucked up the courage and told her about all of my problems, especially the photos that Grandmum had given me. Aunt Sim was horrified! She comforted me and assured me that she would do what she could to help.

Over the next few days, things really started to look up. Aunt Sim dropped subtle hints to my parents on several occasions, and was able to highlight the differences between growing up in India and the UK. She even went as far as to say,

'For Tina I think we should look for a boy from over here.'

I could tell that Grandmum wasn't very happy. She wanted me to marry this one guy called Pavan. I mean, you should have seen his photo! OK, maybe he had a nice personality, according to Grandmum, but he looked awful!

Later Aunt Sim took me to one side,

'Tina, I don't think the topic of getting married in India will crop up again very quickly, so don't worry. I've spoken to your mum and she seems ok about looking for a guy over here.'

I was so relieved; it was one pressure off my mind. Aunt Sim told me that she didn't really suggest a 'love marriage' but said she would be happy to help and show me some guys she knew. I would also have more time to get to know the guy first. I didn't say no to Aunt Sim because I was grateful for her help and I trusted her.

I'd come to accept that as a B.A.G I would one day have an arranged marriage because that's how it was for us. I also knew that my parents weren't going to accept just any guy as their son-in-law. Sooner or later I was going to have to tie the knot with someone, so I thought I should at least try to find a guy that I liked and who my parents could accept.

Soon after, I was introduced to two or three guys, it was a start but they weren't for me. I just wanted to meet a guy who would like me for myself and who wouldn't pretend to be someone he wasn't.

Most of the guys I saw were very self-obsessed. One seemed only interested in going clubbing every night. He even came dressed as if he was about to go out; you know, the baggy shirt and trousers with a thick metal belt reeking of cheap aftershave. Another was the complete opposite he hated going out and was only interested in slobbing out in front of the TV. I believed that because he was what I call 'moto', big. He was three times my size! Even Aunt Sim doubted they would be my type. It seemed that if they had the looks they didn't have the brains and if they had the brains they didn't have the looks. I just couldn't win!

4   Things were progressing slowly so Aunt
     Sim made loads more phone calls to try
     and find me a suitable guy. She arranged
for me to meet someone, telling me truthfully she didn't
know much about him even though it was her friend's
son.

I wasn't exactly overjoyed and Aunt Sim could tell
something was up. So I told her about all the pressure I
had from uni and that I felt I just wasn't ready to marry,
that I wanted mum and dad to wait until I had finished
studying. Aunt Sim reassured me and said that all she
wanted was for me to find someone I would be happy
with, before she had to go back to London. I was grateful
that she understood and was so concerned about my
happiness. I asked her about the guy she wanted me to
see. She said his name was Nikil Kapoor and he was a
computer engineer. He was local and had two sisters,
one of whom was married.

This time I actually made a big effort in getting
dressed up for the meeting. I wore my new outfit, with
matching bangles and bindi. It was a beautiful electric
blue fish-tail lengha covered in sequins. The dupata

dropped neatly off my right shoulder. This time I kept my hair loose. As I came down the stairs Aunt Sim said how beautiful I looked. It was kind of embarrassing all my family there admiring me. Dad then drove us all to Aunt Anisha's house. It was only about ten minutes away. I was dead cold and I could see goose pimples appearing on my arms, even though Aunt Sim had offered me her shawl, I wanted to avoid wearing one because I didn't want to hide my suit.

Fortunately Aunt Anisha's house was warm and cosy. This was my first visit to Aunt Anisha's and she seemed very nice. It was an older style house with really high ceilings. I spent a good few minutes just looking around. She offered all of us a drink and I was glad to receive a hot cup of coffee.

Suddenly the doorbell rang; I could hear voices in the hall. As they walked into the living room my dad got up to shake hands with the guy's father. My mum greeted his mother, I also said hello to her.

I looked around the room and caught sight of the guy I had come to meet. For a few moments I just stood and stared at him, my mouth wide open. He was drop dead gorgeous!

'Hi Rabba!'

Aunt Sim grabbed my arm and pulled me down. It was most embarrassing; I hadn't realized they had all sat down. After that I didn't know where to look, I felt myself blushing.

Mein mar java! You should have seen him! As he sat there in his white shirt I could see the outline of his body. Man was he fit or what? Forget all those other guys I saw, they weren't men, well, not in comparison to this one. He was a right hunk. I couldn't believe he was still single and I didn't know how I was going to speak to him? I was feeling really flustered.

Kasam se! Woh shrabi akiya! I could really drown in those beautiful hazel eyes. Aunt Sim definitely picked well this time! I wished Deepa was there; she would have gone crazy for him too. I knew she would be so jealous when I told about this gorgeous guy I had met. I couldn't keep my eyes off him. I was so pleased I had made the effort to dress up and wear my hair loose.

'Just look at those lips! Can't wait to bite those off!'

'Did you say something Tina?' whispered Aunt Sim.

'No,' I said quickly.

I thought I had better be careful; I had spoken more loudly than I thought. He sat opposite me, he was clean-shaven and I could smell his aftershave, he smelt divine. I could feel my heart pounding in my chest; I'd never experienced this before. My hands were tightly clasped in my lap and I tried counting slowly in my head to calm down but that didn't seem to help.

After a while Aunt Sim took us into another room and briefly introduced us to one another, which I thought was nice. I could feel the chemistry between us; I just knew he was the one. It was love at first sight. As he sat next to me, I felt as if I'd died and gone to Heaven.

We chatted about what we both did and the things we liked, and I felt really comfortable with him. He was very attentive; I loved the way he quickly picked up my bracelet, which he noticed had fallen off my wrist. He had a lovely sense of humour. Slowly I felt more at ease. He was perfect. The best part was we both shared the same interests: music and travel. Suddenly, I noticed I was asking far too many questions, he was grinning at me. I asked whether he had a former girlfriend but he said he didn't. I also asked how religious he was and whether he drank or smoked. Time really flew by and, before I knew it, it was time to leave.

When we got home mum and dad asked me what I thought about Nikil. When I told them I really liked him you should have seen their faces. Grandmum was over the moon and came over and gave me a big hug. This was the second hug I had received since she had been here! Mum and dad were also over the moon. I could tell they were really happy, mum couldn't help but shed a tear. Later on Aunt Sim came over to talk to me about Nikil. I told her how I felt after meeting him and said that I thought he was really nice and caring and I could see her smiling.

'So, you've found Mr. Right have you?' She laughed.
I smiled,
'I think I have.'
'Did you get his phone number?'
'No, but he said he would phone in a few days'.

Aunt Sim was now happy to return to London and asked me to keep her informed about Nikil. While I was sad to see her go, I was also really happy, maybe an arranged marriage wasn't so bad after all.

When she left I gave Aunt Sim a big hug. She promised to keep in touch and said that I should ring her if I needed anyone to talk to.

The only thing on my mind was Nikil. I sat in my bedroom thinking about him. I couldn't understand why he hadn't phoned, he did say a few days and it had nearly been a week!

Time dragged then, finally, Nikil rang and, typically, I was on the loo at the time.

I could hear mum laughing as I ran upstairs to take the call. I was so glad she hadn't mentioned that I was on the loo. Just imagine how embarrassing that would have been!

When I spoke to him I have to say the conversation was very short and dry. He wasn't a bit romantic. He basically informed me that he was taking me out to lunch over the weekend. I was a bit disappointed as I expected him to have made more of an effort; after all, it was the first time we had spoken since we first saw each other. Perhaps he was in a hurry. Anyway the main thing was he had phoned! I told mum that Nikil was coming over and that we were going out for lunch. Dad wasn't too pleased about this but fortunately, mum convinced him to let me go.

I decided not to put on an Asian suit because I didn't know where we were going, so I put on something more casual but still made an effort to look good. As usual, Grandmum, was adding a bit of masala you know fussing about my choice of outfit. When mum asked why I hadn't dressed up in Asian clothes I told her I would look silly if I got dressed up for a casual lunch. I don't think dad was very impressed either. I could hear him mumbling to mum, asking why I was so casual but luckily he didn't make too much of a fuss. I sat in my bedroom looking out of the window, waiting for Nikil.

Finally he arrived. I darted downstairs and just as I reached the last step I heard the doorbell, so I opened the door. He smiled, gave me a lovely bunch of flowers and said how beautiful I looked. I was on cloud nine! I thanked him and asked him in. He went into the living room and started talking to dad and Grandad. While they chatted I went into the kitchen and helped mum get the samosas ready. Mum always cooked samosas for guests. I served them with the samosas and drinks and mum and Grandmum came in to say hello.

We all sat and talked while they ate, I didn't feel I could sit next to him with my dad sitting there although dad and Nikil seemed to be getting along fine. I was hoping Nikil would say that we should get going but he didn't move. I kept looking at the time and occasionally left the room to see if he would get the message that I wanted to leave. I was getting more and more frustrated. How insensitive can a man be? It should be me he is trying to impress. After all, I was the one he was hoping to marry. An hour later he finally said,

'Well we'd better be going'.

Hurray! At last!

As we left I said,

'I didn't think you were going to move?' He just laughed.

He had a lovely smile. I couldn't take my eyes off him. He had a beautiful blue BMW and I commented how nice his car was.

'So, how long have you had this BMW for?'

'Oh not too long, about a year,' Nikil replied.

I could see he loved his car. Everything in the car was so immaculately clean; I could smell polish as I sat in the front seat. He asked where I would like to go but I let him decide. We went for a drive and then we had lunch in a small restaurant. It was nice being alone with Nikil away from the house and family.

'So, where shall we go from here?' Nikil asked me.

'Well, can you see us as a couple?' I replied shyly.

Nikil laughed,

'Um, yeah!'

'Well, I think we should start to get to know each other first, I mean I don't really know you that well yet but so far I like what I see!'

'So you fancy me do you?'

I blushed.

'Well, you have got gorgeous eyes.'

'Have I? I didn't know that,' he smiled.

'Well, you do now!' I said and we burst out laughing.

Over lunch we talked more about whether we liked each other, and agreed that as we did we should tell my mum and dad that we were going to carry on seeing one other.

When we got back to my place Nikil had to leave straightaway, as he had an appointment to keep. I could tell that mum and dad were anxious to find out what had happened between us so I told them that we had decided to continue seeing each other. Dad shouted out,

'Well, we'll have to start making arrangements for the wedding!'

I was shocked. It was only my first proper date with Nikil, weren't they jumping the gun a bit?

'I don't recall myself saying I was getting married'. I argued. 'Dad, we've only just started to get to know each other!' Then mum jumped in.

'Tina, we can't wait a whole year just to see whether you like each other. It doesn't work like that'.

'Then how does it work?' I said,

'Well, do you like him?' said mum.

'Yes, I do'. I replied.

'Then that's all you need to know'.

I was speechless. Next thing I knew, dad was on the phone to Nikil's parents,

'Let's fix a date for the marriage ceremony.'

What could I say? There was nothing left to say. I was engaged!

I tried phoning Nikil just to let him know what dad was doing but he wasn't picking up his phone. So I left a message. He sent me a text telling me not to worry and that he was fine with it.

5   Before Nikil and I could do anything our parents had made the arrangements for our wedding, and the dates for the engagement ceremony were fixed. Nikil and I saw each other every weekend. During our time together we went to the cinema because we loved watching the latest Bollywood films. We also went bowling and on long drives in Nikil's car.

At the engagement ceremony Nikil placed a beautiful heart-shaped engagement ring on my finger. This was official. We were engaged to marry. Life was now looking up for me.

The following day was April Fools' Day. I always played a prank on dad first thing in the morning. This time I set the alarm clock an hour earlier than usual and when dad went into the bathroom and looked at the clock, I could hear him screaming. Man, he nearly killed me!

'Tina, tu mar gayi!'

I quickly ran downstairs, grabbing my post as I left to go to uni.

When I reached the bus stop I started opening my

mail. It was all junk mail but when I opened the last letter, for a second or two everything around me just stopped. It was a poison pen letter. I stood there like a zombie holding it as if it was about to explode in my face. Then, just as suddenly, I snapped out of it. It was an April Fools' joke, of course. How stupid could I be? For a minute Nikil had really sucked me in. Did he really think I was going to fall for it? OK, so I nearly did but I didn't think Nikil would do something like this to me.

I buzzed him on his mobile but there was no answer. Typical. I sent him a text instead saying, 'Very funny Nikil,' and left it at that.

For once someone had played a trick on me and I could now see why dad got so uptight when I played a trick on him every year.

When I got to uni I told Sarah and Michelle about Nikil's prank. They thought it was quite hilarious but Denise thought it was quite a sick joke to play when we were about to get married. She did have a point, it was quite clever what he had done. I mean sticking newspaper words to form a letter was quite tricky. It must have taken him all evening to do something like this. But, as Denise pointed out, what he'd written wasn't very nice either:

LETTER ONE

Your husband to be has a girlfriend.
I've married now but he dated me too.
Don't believe him like the rest.
Hire a detective. He loves her more than anyone.
Do not marry him.

I put the letter into my handbag. I thought that next year I would really make him suffer.

'Just wait Nikil, two can play that game.'

It didn't scare me but I thought the bit about hiring a detective was a bit O.T.T. Come off it; do people still hire detectives over small matters such as this? He really thought he knew how to pull one over me, didn't he?

Nikil rang me later that afternoon. I was in a lecture so I couldn't speak to him for long but I told him that I loved his sick trick. He just denied it all. Did he think I was stupid or something? Well, that's what he was bound to say. I quickly shut the phone off as Dr. Milroy saw me talking.

Everyone was scared of Dr. Milroy. He had these really thick eyebrows. He gave me the creeps. He always wore his long white lab coat and if you talked while he was talking he would come up and put his face right into yours and tell you to get out. No one messed with him. The only good thing about Dr. Milroy was he was a really good lecturer; he explained everything in great detail and gave us lots of handouts, unlike some other lecturers that gave us nothing.

Mum was fuming when I got home. Well, I was a bit late. OK, maybe an hour late, but it wasn't my fault. Denise and Sarah had dragged me to the April Fools' Party, which I told them I wasn't going to go to. I knew mum would go ballistic and as soon as I got home she started yelling,

'Tina, do you know what time this is? It's not good for a girl to be out so late in the evening! Haven't you seen the news lately about girls getting raped?' It was a good job that Dad hadn't arrived home otherwise he would have been on my case too. Can't a girl just have a bit of fun?

When I went into the living room there were lots of bags full of Asian suits and wedding stuff.

'You've been busy Mum.' I said.

'Yes, Grandmum and I have been to Handsworth and they had some lovely things. You should have come.'

'Well, it looks like you've bought the whole shop home with you.'

I noticed a few gold sets on the table, which were nice but not really my style. Mum wanted me to wear one for my wedding but gold didn't really appeal to me. I like simple clothes and thin chains. I hate fobber earrings and all that thick gold piled around my neck. It's just too much. Anyway, I had to choose one set as mum asked me to but because they were all very similar, I asked Grandmum to pick one for me. Mum just looked at me and I knew what that meant. She was wondering why I hadn't chosen it myself.

I sat by Grandad, munching an apple and he chatted to me about when he got married to Grandmum. He said he didn't have any choice; his parents had already chosen Grandmum when he was very small and the marriage took place when he turned sixteen, that was what happened in their day. It was a good job that didn't happen anymore. I found it hard to imagine being fixed up with someone I've never met at such an early age?

6 Everyone was busy preparing for the wedding. As the father of the bride, dad had a lot to do. He had to make arrangements for the hall and sort out the catering and so forth. Traditionally the bride's family made all the arrangements. I didn't agree with this but respected that this was how it had been for so many generations. It must have been quite stressful, but it was nice to see everyone so happy. Grandmum, especially, was over the moon. She wanted everything to be just perfect. Aunt Sim had also come over to help with the wedding preparations. Uncle Jav stayed in London because he had a lot of business to sort out before he could come over again.

Too many late nights talking to Nikil on the mobile and texting him had started to affect me. It was a good job I had finished uni and was now able to relax. I woke up quite late and could hear Grandmum singing wedding songs. It was nice because it reminded me that it would soon be my big day. After showering I went downstairs to the kitchen. Mum had made me some lovely Indian tea. It was nice, a bit spicy, which I liked first thing in the morning. Indian Tea is made by simply boiling some water, adding some teabags and sugar in a saucepan and letting it brew then adding some tea masala and milk to give it a lovely taste.

Mum gave me the post. I opened my letters while I ate my breakfast. I suddenly noticed one of the letters, which was underneath the first. It looked very similar to the one I had received on April Fools' Day. I looked at the back of the envelope to see if there was a name of the sender but there wasn't but it did have a Birmingham postmark. Feeling a little confused I opened it. The letter was folded in half. I looked at it and was horrified. It was another letter like the one I had received on April Fools' Day except it was hand written this time. I sat there, absorbing everything it said. I was now very concerned about who had sent the first letter. Maybe it wasn't an April Fools' joke after all. Mum asked me if I was OK, I just shook my head and took the letter upstairs to my bedroom.

I read it again carefully, it said:

LETTER TWO

To Miss Sinhasi,

You may have taken the first letter as a joke but I am only trying to warn you. Your husband to be has a long-term lover who he is still seeing. He has been involved with her for a long time. He is only marrying you to keep his parents happy because his family is very united, although he probably will not admit it. He will be with her at every opportunity your back is turned.

Nikil dated me a long time ago and I did not want to leave him, but I had to have an arranged marriage due to family pressures. I'm happily married now. He is always with his girlfriend; he is very clever at skipping from place to place at all times of the day without anyone even noticing.

Don't you smell her perfume on him when he meets you? They are often spotted together by my husband and I, and also some of my friends. Do you really want to be second best? Just think, how often does he come to see you? Does he telephone you morning, noon and night? Does he get close to you? He is madly in love with her. He buys her everything. I am not jealous although I admit he is very good looking, well dressed, kind hearted and lots of fun to be with.

I am happily married now but I know how I would feel if my husband had someone else. I would not marry a man like that. Be warned, you will thank me one day.

This time I began to wonder whether Nikil was actually hiding something from me. The letter was definitely warning me not to marry him and I was now seriously worried. The person writing the letter was right, how close did he get to me? I mean during our time together we were close but so far Nikil hadn't touched me, let alone hold my hand. I stopped, was I getting sucked into this letter a bit too much? Maybe it was just a big hoax. Nikil didn't seem to be hiding anything from me. It didn't really make sense because we got on really well when we were together. There were no signals from Nikil to suggest that he didn't want to marry me. I had to try and find out who was sending these letters.

I phoned Nikil and luckily, he picked up his mobile. I told him about both letters and that I'd realized he hadn't sent the first letter after all. How stupid could I have been to believe Nikil had played a prank on me?

When he came over later that day we went out and discussed the letters in his car. He sat gazing at them before looking me in the eyes and telling me that he had never had a girlfriend before. He said he was just as confused and couldn't understand who had written them.

'Tina, I don't know who's behind these letters, all I can say is that I have nothing to do with it,' he said in a quiet voice.

'I'm not saying its you Nikil, but I am really scared, the wedding isn't too far away and this isn't a good sign to start a relationship is it?' I replied.

'Look, I've never had a girlfriend before, just trust me!'

Nikil sounded irritated and he sat in his seat fiddling with his car keys.

'You are the first guy I have actually been with. You know how it is. I just don't want any problems after we're married. I haven't even told mum and dad about these letters. I don't want everyone going crazy about some hoax letters. I know my dad would flip if he heard what I was getting in the post!'

'I'm glad you've kept it quiet, there's no point telling everyone when we can sort it out between us.'

He reassured me and suggested that I just put the letters in the bin and try to forget all about it. He seemed pleased when I told him that no one else knew about these letters because I didn't want everyone to start to worrying.

Maybe he was right. If he said he was single then I

should have believed him, shouldn't I? So, I left it at that. Maybe someone out there was dead jealous; after all, Nikil was gorgeous. Anyone would kill to have him. If he could do jadoo like this on me then he could do it to anyone.

I hid the letters under my bed and forgot about them. I didn't want to bin them at this precise moment because I still had a bit of doubt in my mind. I didn't know whether I was reading a bit too much between the lines but why hadn't Nikil touched me? We were engaged and usually in the car I held his hand as we sat talking, he never made the first move. Maybe being an Asian, he was holding back. Being with a guy for the first time even I didn't know how far I should go with him. I dare not kiss him before marriage as it wasn't right. I wanted it to be special for our Suhaag Raat.

I felt uncomfortable talking about it with him. I mean when I did sit near him my heart was always racing 100mph and my hands would go all sweaty. He would come loaded up with aftershave and as I sat in the car all I could smell was his aftershave. It was such a gorgeous smell I sometimes felt like just grabbing him, but that wouldn't happen. I was too shy to even move an inch.

Dad and Grandad sat in the living room watching cricket. I couldn't really see the fascination about cricket. Nikil loved cricket too. You should have seen the three of them when they got together. Anyway, as I showed some interest in cricket because of Nikil I actually started liking the game. India and Pakistan were playing each other. It was exciting and Tendulkar was really great. I thought he played really well.

I now had lots of spare time on my hands. All I was waiting for was my uni results. I was hoping that I had passed with at least a second class honours. I knew I wouldn't get a first but I had high hopes about getting a 2:1.

I actually felt excited now that I was getting married. Nerves were kicking off at the thought that I would soon be called Mrs Kapoor and I had forgotten all about the letters.

Aunt Sim and I were spending loads of time together. We were having girly chats and spending loads of money on new outfits. It was just great! She wanted me to have the best wedding ever. My dad was sorting out all the catering. Mum was busy sorting out all the other wedding preparations; placing orders for the flowers and things like that. Everything was going along very smoothly.

7

Nikil and I were spending loads of time together. Mum and Dad didn't mind me seeing Nikil now that we were about to get married. The more time I spent with Nikil the closer we were getting. I have to say I was deeply in love with the guy. I never thought I would fall in love in this way. He was definitely my man. We spent hours going on long drives and looking at posh houses. I'm sure Nikil was thinking about buying a house for us. At the moment he was living with his parents but from the way he talked I got the impression he was thinking of moving out after we married. I didn't want to ask him directly but I was quite sure that was what he had in mind.

Mum was calling me. I could hear her shouting,

'Tina get up! It's nearly ten'. I couldn't believe it. I had a hair appointment at eleven! I quickly got up, got dressed and went downstairs.

'Tina there's a letter for you,' said Mum.

'I'll look at it later', I replied. 'I've got to go to town to have my hair done'.

Aunt Sim was going with me. Mum handed me the letter as we left. As I took the letter I did a double-take,

I recognized the envelope. I was petrified. Not again; it couldn't be! Was it another mystery letter, like the others? I didn't want to open it in front of Aunt Sim, so I shoved it in my handbag. Aunt Sim asked who the letter was from but I couldn't tell her. I lied and said it was from Deepa.

After having my hair done we went around, window-shopping but I couldn't concentrate. My mind was on the letter, which was still unopened in my bag. What could that person have written?

Just before lunch we headed back home. By now I was dying to see what it said but I couldn't open it while Aunt Sim was there. She asked why I was quiet but I was able to reassure her that I was OK. When she left I quickly sneaked upstairs. I was right; it *was* another mystery letter! I was getting really scared and was worried about what this person had written. What if they were telling me the truth? Was I reading too much into it? But then maybe Nikil was right: it was just a hoax. Oh, I was really messed up and just didn't know how to handle it. I knew Nikil would tell me to ignore them, but how did I know he wasn't lying to me? Maybe I should have told someone. I looked at the other two letters that I had received. All of them said the same thing: that Nikil had a girlfriend. This time the person had written:

LETTER THREE

To Tina

So did you have courage to confront him? What did he say? Did he admit to anything? Has he telephoned you to convince you to marry him? I do not think he will try to convince you, he will try in front of his parents, but he really wants his girlfriend.

His girlfriend still meets him and you could get more evidence by hiring a detective. We have seen them together more and more in the last few weeks. I am sure you will see that I am only trying to help you.

You will thank me one day. He will never love you as much as her. His family will run your life. He is a smooth talker and will impress most people. He will marry you but he will still meet and love her. He has plenty of opportunities to sneak out and meet her.

If you decide to continue with him then you will realize what a mistake you have made. He doesn't really want you!

Well, I could tell from the exclamation mark at the end of the letter, that the person wasn't very happy about me seeing Nikil. I mean, it definitely sounded like it was from a girl. It looked like she wasn't happy that I hadn't said no yet. Why was this person so adamant about me getting a detective? The wedding was getting really close and the arrangements had been sorted. Should I really kick up a fuss now? Man, this was all bad timing. My parents had paid for all the catering, the hall and invitations. If I said no now, what a waste of money this would all be. What if Nikil wasn't to blame for any of this?

Denise rang me on the mobile; she wanted me to meet her up in the coffee shop in town. She was messed up: her boyfriend had told her he had finished with her. I had to meet her, so I grabbed my jacket and told Mum that I would be back soon. Mum was too busy to say no. She had a few relatives over and they were in their own little world.

When I got to town Denise was in a bad state. I had never seen her like this before. She told me what had happened, about how Richard had been sleeping with Michelle from uni. I felt really sorry for her. She'd been seeing Richard for two and a half years. At the same time, I was having bad vibes about Nikil too. I hoped my situation wasn't going to turn out like Denise's. I wanted to tell Denise about the letters but she had her own problems. As for Sarah she had gone to London, Deepa was now pregnant and Rani had gone to the States with her family. So, there was no one I could really talk to. I wasn't sure whether I should tell Aunt Sim or not. What if she told dad and they decided to call the wedding off? Things would really get messed up.

When I got home, mum dragged me into the kitchen. 'Tina, I need to talk to you.'

I could see from her expression she was dead serious. What did she want to tell me? Had something happened? Then she showed me the letters. They were the mystery letters. Suddenly my heart started pounding. How did she get hold of them? I questioned her about where she had found the letters but Mum was getting really uptight. I told her everything about the first letter up to the last. She was totally gobsmacked.

When dad came home she told him everything. Dad went mad. The wedding day was very near. He picked up the phone and rang Nikil's dad. I was getting really worried. Then Nikil arrived with his parents. Grandmum and grandad hadn't got a clue what all the fuss was about. It all happened so suddenly.

Dad was having a go at Nikil, questioning him about the letters. Nikil didn't look at all pleased and he convinced dad that he hadn't got anything to do with them.

'Look dad, I don't know who's been sending these letters to Tina but none of its true!' said Nikil.

'How can you say that?' Shouted dad.

'Please calm down, my son isn't like that. He is always at home after he finishes work. He hardly goes out in the evenings.'

'I have a daughter, what if he is lying?'

'I know you are worried but we want Tina to be happy with Nikil. We have two daughters too. So I can understand what you are saying. The wedding is very near now and the invitations have all been sent out, is it really worth calling the wedding off over some prank letters?'

Dad calmed down, he looked at Nikil and said

'Ok, I am trusting you.'

'You won't regret this Mr Sinhasi.' said Nikil's dad as he put his hand on his shoulder.

Well, it was too late for me to kick up a fuss. As usual, it was all brushed under the carpet, you know, the Indian way.

I decided to put the letters aside after this incident. I didn't really want to spoil everything now. For all I knew the letters were written by a jealous girl who may have loved Nikil to bits. Dad told me to ignore any more letters if they came. I thought it was the best thing to do now, after all, I loved Nikil so much that I didn't want to break it off just over a few stupid letters. If he said he had nothing to do with them, then I should believe him.

One day before the wedding, just when everyone's nerves were really kicking off, I received not one but two more letters. But I knew it was too late now. I had to take a gamble. My heart told me to marry Nikil and that's what I intended to do. I knew deep down there were a lot of unanswered questions but it was too late. Maybe I would never know who had written those letters. I decided not to tell mum and dad about the last two letters because it would cause more tension, on top of the final wedding preparations. Mum was already in a bad state; I could hear her telling Grandmum that she was going to miss me. I felt really sad inside too. I would be leaving the family home. It was a big, and scary step. New people, a new home, and you know you can't act the way you want to when you're not at your family home. On top of it I would have to get up early and wear traditional Indian clothes. It was definitely going to be a challenge.

Well, after all the fuss with the letters I had now given up on them. They weren't going to come in the way of my big day. The next day was a new beginning and I wanted to leave those letters behind once and for all before I went and lived with Nikil. I know you are going to be curious about what they said. The first one just repeated itself about why Nikil was marrying me:

LETTER FOUR

To Tina

Have you questioned him again? What did he say? Has he begged you to stay with him or does he say that he has nothing or anyone to hide? He has to say that he has nobody else because his family would be brought to shame. Has he ever said that he loves you or does he ever touch you? He and his girlfriend are inseparable. They cannot leave each other alone. Do you or his family know where he was on certain days at certain times? He was with his girlfriend. She also has a car so she can meet him.

Nikil cannot disappoint his family so that is the reason he is marrying you. His sister is also involved with someone of another religion but the family does not know.

I am not joking or playing around. I also do not have an interest in Nikil. If you trust him or believe what he is saying then you are a fool and you will regret marrying him. Does he show interest in you or anything? I know certain dates and times when he has been with her. If you are religious ask your god about Nikil. Nikil must be feeling guilty about what he is doing to you. The final decision has to be down to you.

That was the first of the two letters I received. I have to say I couldn't get them out of my head. I kept thinking whether I had made the right decision. It was now too late to even say no. But I couldn't say no to Nikil. I was madly in love with him. He made me so happy and I didn't want to lose that. I loved every little thing about him. But the letters were so convincing I just couldn't think straight anymore.

The final letter said much the same again but was worded differently. If there were photos then I could have understood but there were only letters. There was nothing else to go on. I was sick of reading all this garbage about Nikil and his supposed girlfriend.

On occasions when Nikil and I were together I

mentioned the letters but he wasn't very happy. He asked me if I trusted him. I felt really bad. I did trust him but I just couldn't help thinking what the letters had said. If he did have a girlfriend I'm sure he wouldn't even bother looking at marrying another girl. There weren't any signs that made me doubt Nikil even for a second. He talked well with my parents and he was chatty and friendly with me. So why should I doubt him? The final letter repeated itself again, it said,

LETTER FIVE

To Tina

Do you still trust him? If so you must be easily led by your religious ways. I am not trying to destroy your marriage but just trying to warn you about what lies ahead of you. I saw Nikil and his girlfriend at a secret place one evening last week but I did not have a camera with me. I also saw them elsewhere the weekend before during the afternoon.

I also know of their secret meetings at various times during the evenings. I would have warned you a long time ago but I didn't have the courage but now I think I must warn you and I thought he would have left her by now. Did you know that he even asked one of his previous girlfriends to marry him but she refused because of family problems? How will you feel when you find out he is seeing someone else after you are married?

I know a lot more about Nikil.

Does he love you?

What would you have done if you were in my shoes? Would you have said 'no' just because of a few letters?

The thing is, if you don't trust one another how can a relationship work? To me trust means everything. If I couldn't trust Nikil before the wedding what would it be like while we were married? I had to trust him. Why? Well because I was madly in love with the guy. When you just want to be with someone everything around you just doesn't matter anymore. Even letters like these can seem like nothing.

I had made my decision now and I had to stick with it. There was no turning back. The wedding was taking place and I had to put all this business of the letters behind me. I wanted to enjoy the wedding not feel that I had doubts about him. That wouldn't be a good start would it?

8   It was my big day. I was up early and Denise, Sarah and Rani had come to help get me ready. I was dead excited. It was like a dream come true. I thought how, in a few hours time, Nikil and I would finally be together forever. I couldn't help smiling. The decorations were so nicely done and my outfit was really beautiful. It was a gold embroidered lengha. I felt like a princess in Heaven. It wasn't heavy or uncomfortable, just nice and light. I could remember the trouble we went through just to get this lengha. The man in the shop wouldn't sell it to us because someone had placed a deposit on it. My heart was set on this particular lengha. Then my dad bribed the man by giving him a bit more cash just so that I could have it. I know it was wrong but I just had to have it.

Denise and Sarah filled me in about how the hall was absolutely packed up with people. I was dead nervous. I got even more nervous when Nikil arrived. Sarah and Denise came screaming into the changing room.

'Man, he looks so hot Tina, you lucky devil.' Said Denise.

'Just a few more hours,' said Rani, 'and he's all yours. I can't get over his body!'

'Man, is he fit or what?' added Sarah.

Then, I was finally taken out in the open. All I could see were flashes from the camera. The photographer kept saying,

'Tina, can you look here?' and, 'Tina can you turn your head?'

It was great. I never had this much attention before. I had this heavy garland around my neck, and I felt like I was tilting on one side. I could hear people saying that Nikil had arrived. Everyone had gone to greet them at the entrance of the hall. Then Nikil was brought onto the stage where I was sitting. A long sheet of cloth held by two brothers separated us. The priest gave Nikil my hand under this cloth and he continued with the ceremony. Finally, we tied the knot. The hall was so packed with people that I couldn't think straight. I said my farewells to my family. A white limousine was waiting outside and the driver took us to Nikil's house.

It was my first visit to his house. After the visitors had all gone, Nikil was still very busy socializing with all his mates. I felt quite uncomfortable, left alone without any company. I was also bursting to go to the loo but there wasn't a female in sight. So I ended up asking my father-in-law! That was so embarrassing. Finally Nikil's younger sister, Pooja, took me to his bedroom. Well, it was my Suhaag Raat and his two sisters had decorated his bedroom beautifully. It was the four posts all decorated with flowers and a big red piece of material draped on the top. It looked really romantic. I never imagined that my Suhaag Raat would be like this. The bed had rose petals and rice all over it. Nikil's older sister, Neha, told me to wait in the room for him. My head was covered as they do, you know, like in the Indian films. Then I heard Nikil coming. I felt really nervous now.

This was it: my reunion with my love. That feeling, it's just so great you cannot imagine. Then he came in and sat by me. Just then there was a big noise. I burst out laughing; apparently someone had left a soft horn under the bed sheets, so when Nikil sat down he sat on the horn. It was hilarious. Nikil went red with embarrassment. I could hear them all laughing outside. 'Go on Nikil!' shouted the youngsters. Nikil cleared the bed, which had other obstacles hidden inside it. It was like a game to them – two lovers on their first night.

Nikil slowly started taking off my jewellery. His hands were nice and warm and I felt all funny inside. He brushed his hands on the side of my face and I could feel the warmth of his love. As he came so close to kiss me I was getting really nervous. I started asking him stupid questions until he said, 'Shh!' Then, that was it; we enjoyed our first night together. It was the best day of my life!

The next day we had an early start because we were going on our honeymoon. Nikil kept it all quiet until we got to the airport. When he showed me the tickets and I found out that we were off to Dubai for two whole weeks, man, you should have seen me! I jumped on him and started kissing him. Dubai! I had always wanted to go there. I was just so happy. The plane trip was really enjoyable. We had first class seats. I was given a bunch of flowers by one of the stewardesses to congratulate us on our marriage, which was really nice.

When we landed in Dubai I could feel the heat. It was going to be really hot. As we arrived I was given a bunch of flowers as a welcome. Nikil had booked one of the top hotels and the quality was out of this world. Everyone was so polite and helpful. The food was presented beautifully and was absolutely delicious. We spent a lot of time touring and looking around and were chauffeur driven everywhere we went. The buildings were remarkable; I had never seen anything like them before. We had such a fantastic honeymoon; it was truly unforgettable.

All too soon we were back home. I was partly glad to be home because I wanted to come home and tell everyone what a lovely time we had had. Nikil took loads of photos and I couldn't wait to get them developed to show my friends. Nikil's mum and his two sisters went to a lot of trouble, preparing a welcome home party for us and had cooked some tasty Indian spicy dishes.

After the party we visited mum and dad. You should have seen them all. They were so happy. Dad, Grandad and Nikil sat and talked whilst, Grandmum, mum and I talked. I had lots to tell them. When it was time for us to leave, mum was in tears again. It must have been hard that I wasn't living there anymore. She knew I was happy, so I knew she would soon get used to it.

Back at Nikil's house I started to tackle the mountain of washing that we had brought back from our honeymoon. Then Nikil told me that he was going away for a week to London, which shocked me. Why hadn't he told me this before? He said he had only just found out so after a while I came around. Nikil's mum wasn't too pleased either because we had only just arrived back from our honeymoon but I told her it was OK. I asked Nikil for his hotel details in London but he said he didn't know them because his friend was sorting out the accommodation for him. He said that his friend was going to text them to him later and I asked Nikil to ring and pass on his details to me when he reached his hotel.

I felt quite uncomfortable without Nikil. It was OK when he was there but, because I knew he was off for a week, I wasn't sure how I was going to spend all that time with his parents. Anyway, I had decided to go job-hunting during the day as I now needed a job. The first letter addressed to 'Mrs Tina Kapoor' was my exam results. I kept my fingers crossed as I opened it. I had passed with an upper second class honours. I was so happy. I phoned everyone telling them the good news. I phoned Nikil but as usual I couldn't get through to him, but I didn't leave a message, as I wanted to tell him myself.

I was disappointed that Nikil hadn't phoned. I must have tried a hundred times but for some reason he wasn't picking up the phone. The following day he rang me. I was quite angry with him but I soon calmed down. I told him that I had passed my degree and he congratulated me and promised we'd celebrate when he got back.

While Nikil was in London my mother-in-law was really nice to me. Actually, the time alone without Nikil was good because it gave me a chance to bond with his parents. I felt more at ease and at home, which was nice.

Nikil's younger sister had gone abroad to Switzerland with a few of her friends so it was just me at home with Nikil's parents.

I spent a lot of time in the bedroom while his mum and dad watched TV. I quite liked the bedroom; it was small but very cosy. There were lots of teddy bears and unusual gifts on the window ledge and dressing-table. I noticed they all had the initials MC scribbled on the back of them. I didn't know what that meant; maybe it was from a friend or cousin of Nikil's.

We had loads of relatives coming to visit us. None of them knew that Nikil had gone to London. They all seemed very nice but, you know how it is with some of the older ladies, they can't help butting in and finding something to gossip about. So I got some stupid remarks about why Nikil hadn't taken me to London, why he couldn't cancel his appointments and all that rubbish. They all made jokes about Nikil being away at this time. I could understand their point but if he had to go, that wasn't his fault was it?

I spent the week applying for different posts and, luckily, I managed to score an interview at the place I did my work placement. A career was the only thing I felt was lacking in my life. Everything else I had. It sounds quite basic, doesn't it, but I was truly happy.

9

When Nikil arrived home, I told him how much I had missed him while he was away. I must have rung him four times a day. I wished he had done the same but I couldn't blame him when he had work to do. After all, I had all the time in the world and the poor thing was working all week.

I cooked some lovely Indian dishes, which I knew he would love. Nikil's mum and dad had gone shopping when he arrived. My mother-in-law had told me to eat with Nikil after he had got back. But after putting in all that effort he just threw it back in my face. He had already eaten and, when I asked him to eat, he bluntly refused. He didn't even have the decency to ask if I had eaten. I was really shocked. I couldn't understand what kind of mood he had come back with from London. I thought he may have had an argument at work with some colleagues and so I didn't question him or push him. I decided to leave it at that. He was bound to cool down sooner or later. There was very little communication between us and I was so upset that I went to sleep on an empty stomach.

The next morning I received a phone call saying I had succeeded in the interview and that I had been appointed as Education Welfare Officer. I was over the moon. I was really pleased and gave Nikil the good news. As usual he didn't respond well and I was disappointed with his reaction - he could have made a bit of effort in showing he was happy for me.

Over the next few days Nikil didn't cool down at all. In fact when I asked him about doing things together, he refused and showed no interest. He even asked me to go to my parents' house alone and that he would meet me there later on as he had to deal with something urgently. He didn't show up until very late that evening. It was bad enough that I had to make my own way there but, when he didn't turn up till late, I felt very angry. I told my parents that he had to go somewhere important but I could tell from their faces they knew I was making excuses just to cover for him. Mum and dad didn't say much to Nikil but I could tell that they were appalled at his rudeness.

I told my parents that my new job was going really well. I really enjoyed going to work. The boss had already outlined what a good performance I had made. I had also made good friends with a colleague named Jenny Taylor. Working together in different projects engaged us to get closer. To be honest, each day as I left Nikil's house to go to work I felt that I could breathe again. I just felt I was suffocating in the house with everything that was happening between us.

Since Nikil had come back from London things had changed. I had never seen this side of him before, it was as if he hated me all of a sudden. He was acting so weirdly. If the mobile rang and I was in the room, he would take the call outside. He never did that before. He acted quite normally in front of his parents so that they didn't notice that his behaviour towards me had changed.

I was so upset with him that I phoned Aunt Sim. I just needed someone to talk to. Aunt Sim explained that maybe he was under pressure at work. She told me that men hated telling their wives about their problems and, as a result, they acted a bit strange. Aunt Sim told me not to take it to heart. She was sure that he would come around soon. Maybe she was right. Maybe he was told something about his job, which he was worried about. I thought I'd wait and see if his behaviour changed over the next few weeks. Maybe I was jumping the gun a bit. I mean relationships do have their ups and downs, don't they?

The day of my graduation arrived. I had enough tickets to take Nikil, my mum, dad, my Grandparents and Nikil's family. Nikil had gone out early in the morning after his friend rang him. His mum told him to be back in time to take everyone to the graduation. There was no sign of him and I made loads of calls to his mobile. In the end Nikil's dad had to take us, as he was really worried that I wouldn't get there on time. All the way to the university I felt tearful. What was I going to say to mum and dad?

My parents had already arrived well before us. Mum questioned why I was so late. I didn't say much. She knew something wasn't right and she kept quiet. Dad asked where Nikil was, and his dad sort of laughed and said,

'We don't know where he's got to.'

Dad was really angry, especially when the time of the graduation came and Nikil didn't show up to share the joy with me. Nikil's dad was trying so hard to contact him on the mobile but he just wasn't answering. Sarah and Denise had come and were also asking questions about where my hubby had disappeared to, but I didn't want them to know at this point that I was having problems. I wanted to sort them out for myself first.

As we were about to leave Nikil walked in. My parents were so mad that they gave him the cold shoulder. I couldn't help letting a tear out and just ignored him and walked towards the car. I could hear Nikil's dad questioning him about where he was but he made no apology as to why he hadn't shown up.

I didn't sleep well after that. The gap between us was widening every day and I couldn't help thinking why or what was causing it. I knew deep down that there was a problem in the marriage. I also felt that Nikil didn't love me the way I loved him. I didn't want to think like this because I didn't want to lose Nikil. I felt very obsessed and just wanted to hang onto him. Divorce was something I was totally against. I just had to try hard to make Nikil mine and I knew that wasn't going to be easy, especially after the way he was treating me.

I noticed each time I visited my mum and dad that they had been talking about Nikil and it was obvious that they had started to dislike him for the way he was treating me. I didn't complain to them, after all that's not what parents want to hear when they give a daughter away. I tried very hard to look happy although, underneath it all, I was deeply hurt. My grandparents had gone back to India; and mum and dad were feeling a bit lonely without anyone around.

Things didn't get any better. Over Christmas Nikil was given two tickets to go to a Christmas party from work. I had seen the tickets in his drawer while I was getting my diary out. When I asked him about the Christmas party, to my surprise, he said he had only one ticket. I couldn't understand why he didn't want me to go along with him. I really thought he would take me with him. When I looked again for the other ticket, I noticed he had taken it.

He began leaving small notes on the dressing table saying things like 'I'll see you at 10.00pm' or 'Can you make your own way and I'll see you there?' I couldn't understand why there was a need for this but I didn't question him. I also noticed he had stopped wearing his wedding ring. When I questioned him he said that he wasn't allowed to wear any rings at work due to the type of job he did. I didn't feel too concerned because I trusted him, he was my husband. I couldn't imagine him cheating or deceiving me in any way.

10 Our relationship was steadily deteriorating. I spent most of my time alone. Luckily, I had a job that I could escape to, so time passed by fairly quickly for me. Nikil's mum asked me what was wrong with us two but I said I didn't know. I told her Nikil was acting very strangely and she told me that she would speak to him. The same day I spoke to my mother in law about Nikil's behaviour she mentioned it to him while we were eating and the response he gave was not convincing enough for his parents to believe there was a problem between the two of us.

While I was alone, my mind went back several times to those letters I had received in the post. Maybe that person was telling the truth after all. I still had those letters somewhere at my parents' house but I couldn't recall exactly where I'd hidden them. Even after mum had spoken to Nikil about his behaviour, nothing made any difference until the day I found something I wasn't supposed to find.

Nikil was at work and I was at home cleaning the bedroom. I dropped my earring under the bed and as I reached under the bed to pull it out an envelope appeared. I picked it up and looked at it. It was an ordinary brown envelope but I hadn't seen it before. I opened it to see what it was and as I did my heart broke into a thousand pieces. It was something I wish I had never found. But it was now in my hand and I couldn't put it back as though it didn't exist. The fact was that it did exist and it was Nikil's girlfriend!

The envelope contained photos of Nikil and his girlfriend and Valentine cards. I had never seen her before. I don't really know what he saw in her, she wasn't what I would call good looking. In fact I thought I looked ten times better than her. She was just a skinny girl about twenty-one-years-old, with scruffy long hair. The love letters were all from her, Marie Cooper. The photos weren't just of them standing together but were close up photos of them holding each other and holding hands, that sort of thing. It now clicked to me what MC on the teddy bears and other gifts in the room stood for. That 'dragon' had sent them.

For about ten minutes I couldn't think straight. I never thought I'd see this day. I could feel my hands trembling. I didn't know what to do or say, I had to tell someone and his parents would be the first to know because it was their son that was doing the dirty on me. I pulled myself together, but I couldn't stop my tears from coming. It was my worst nightmare! I could hear Nikil's mum and dad talking in the living room. I walked in and Nikil's mum saw tears in my eyes and rushed towards me,

'What's wrong, Beti?'

I angrily placed the photos in front of them.

'What's all this, mum and dad?' I shouted.

Nikil's dad suddenly went quiet. He picked up the photos and took a closer look. His mum went closer to Nikil's dad to look at the photos. Suddenly his dad started crying very loudly. It was as if he was letting all his pain out. He was disgusted. I mean, Nikil was their only son. I could understand how he must have been feeling, but what about my pain? I was married to him. I had promised to live with him for the rest of my life. It wasn't like an exam where I could just walk out of it if I chose. This was commitment. I mean, I had signed to say he would be my husband. How was I going to solve this problem? There was no way out.

'I've only been married 8 weeks, what am I going to do?

'I don't know what to say Tina, I can't believe our son has turned out like this, please forgive us.'

'We will sort this out Tina beti, please stop crying.' Nikil's mum hugged me, I could see tears coming from her eyes too.

'Wait till Nikil gets home!' shouted dad angrily.

'You told me so many times dad that Nikil wasn't like that, so why am I in this mess?'

His dad stood crying in the living room. I also sat crying, feeling totally helpless.

I told them that I had found love letters and cards, which his girlfriend had written. I told them that the room we slept in had gifts from her. The love letters were all from Marie. After his parents had calmed down, his dad reassured me that he would speak to Nikil as soon as he arrived from work.

When Nikil finally arrived his dad took me into the

living room and told Nikil to come inside for a chat. Then he placed the photos in front of him. Nikil, astonished, looked at me with a horrified look on his face. Then he started shouting,

'She's dead! Why is she making such an issue about it? She had cancer. We were good friends, that's all!'

His dad screamed across the room,

'Nikil stop that rubbish! Just admit she was your girlfriend. You told Tina you didn't have a girlfriend.'

But he denied it all and ran outside with his keys. His dad caught up with him and stopped him from going. He told Nikil to forget the photos and start afresh with me. He said his duty was with me, not this other girl. Nikil agreed but I think he was just pleasing his parents so that they got off his case. That night Nikils dad made Nikil remove all the presents Marie Cooper had given him.

I really wanted to tell mum and dad about the photos but I was worried about what the outcome would be as a result of all this. I knew dad would flip and would take me home without resolving anything. Mum's health hadn't been very good lately and I didn't want to put more pressure on her. I didn't want to end the marriage, I just wanted Nikil to put all this behind him and start afresh with me. I was scared, if I told Aunt Sim she would tell mum and dad and then they may tell me to come back home. I wasn't going to give up that easy. For the time being I decided to keep it all quiet.

11

The next few days Nikil put a bit of effort into the relationship. Nothing romantic, but he took me out here and there. For a while we were getting along fine, well, that's what I thought. Then, one day he did something, which completely killed my love for him.

I had gone to work as usual. When I came home I went upstairs to have a quick shower. I took off my watch and placed it on the dressing table. As I did I saw a small note with my name on it. I picked it up.

Tina
I cannot take it any longer. Look after my grandparents and tell my parents.

I read it several times but somehow it wasn't getting through to my brain. I sat down on the bed. My heart starting pounding loudly and, once again, I felt scared and alone. I then opened his wardrobe and noticed he had taken all his belongings. I ran downstairs with tears in my eyes. His mum was in the kitchen. I called her outside because his Grandad was sitting in the kitchen reading a newspaper.

'Mum look!' She looked at the note. She was totally shocked. Nikil's mum insisted I didn't mention anything in front of her parents because of Grandad's health not being very good as he had just come out of hospital. She told me she didn't want anything happening to her dad and that news like this would just kill him. She asked me to stay quiet for Grandad's sake.

What the hell! Didn't she care how I felt? I was in such a dilemma that I just couldn't say anything. She soon sent Grandad away and then came back to me. Was Nikil's mum more concerned about her dad's health but what about me? Ok I wasn't ill but my husband had just done a runner on me and she expected me to sit back and take it! I felt I couldn't hide anything more from my parents; I had to tell them.

'Dad, it's me Tina,' I whispered as I spoke in to the phone.

'Hi beti, how are you?'

'Dad, he's gone.'

'Who's gone Tina?'

'Nikil has run away and left me dad,' I cried and cried on the phone.

'Tina, I'm coming just wait I will be over right now with your mum.'

I put the phone down and sat there with my head down on my knees.

My parents came over straight away after I rang them to tell them what had happened. Nikil's dad was in a right state. He collapsed a few times while my mum and dad were sitting there. My dad couldn't say much because of the way Nikil's dad was reacting. My mother-in-law was also in great shock about what had happened. Out of common decency and sympathy I stayed at my in-laws' place and looked after them, as they were both in a very bad state.

I needed comfort too. I was totally stressed out and with everything happening to me I felt I had to be the strong one to pick up the pieces to keep Nikil's parents happy. I really hated him. How insensitive could someone be?

The following day I went to his workplace to find out how much holiday he had booked, to give me some idea as to how long he might have gone away for. But, to my shock, Nikil no longer worked there! The people he worked with were not aware that Nikil had even been married, he hadn't told them and he never wore his wedding ring. It now clicked why Nikil had started to leave all these small notes: because he didn't want me to contact him at his workplace because he knew he wouldn't be there! I couldn't believe that each morning he would get dressed as if he was going to work when really he was seeing that witch! As the days went on, I became so upset that I couldn't sleep and so my parents asked me to come home again.

I wasn't the same Tina when I came home. Everything seemed different. I felt alone, heartbroken, and I just couldn't pull myself together. I mean, as a girl you never think that you may have to return to your parental home because of something like this happening, and it's never the same when you do have to return. Everything seems very different and you feel you no longer belong there. Every day tears just fell from my eyes. I couldn't control them. The more I thought, the worse I got. People were talking as well, which didn't help matters. Mum and dad were lying to protect me, telling them that I had just come to visit.

Going to work was the only thing that kept me going. There was times when I broke down at work but luckily Jenny was there to comfort me. Jenny was a good listener and I felt I could talk to her about my problems. I felt the weight had been lifted off my shoulders after speaking to her. She was the only one I felt I could speak to about Nikil, and she always made an effort to spend time with me after work and at weekends.

It was obvious people knew something was wrong. I avoided going out as much as possible, just so that I didn't bump into anyone I knew. I managed to find those mystery letters that I had received before I had married Nikil. I spent hours looking at them. Everything written was damn true! How stupid could I have been? Why didn't I listen to my gut instincts? Why did I let my heart make the decision? There was no point in looking at these letters now, the damage had been done. There was no turning back. I had to face whatever was going to come now. Now I understood why they say love is blind. That's how it was when I was in love with Nikil. I was so crazy about him that I shut everything out just so that I could be with him. If only I could go back in time.

Well, after two weeks of going to hell and back we finally got a phone call. It was Nikil's dad. He spoke to dad to say that Nikil had come home the previous day. He said that Nikil was in a bad state but would be coming over to sort everything out. When dad told me, I was horrified. I hated him so much; I just didn't want to see him. Did Nikil think everything was going to be OK by apologizing? I didn't think so. Did I really want to see his ugly face?

When they turned up Nikil looked really bad. He had big bags under his eyes as though he hadn't slept for ages. I thought there was no way I was going to give him an easy ride.

'Tina, Nikil is really sorry,' said his dad.

'We want you to come home and start again with Nikil.'

I sat there with mum and dad, not saying a single word

'He's treated her so badly how can you even suggest Tina goes back to him? What kind of husband does he think he is? Didn't I tell you?'

Nikil's dad looked ashamed and appalled with what had happened.

'I'm sorry Tina.'

I looked up; he could barely look me in the eye. I stayed quiet not knowing what to say or do.

Dad was really getting hot and I knew soon he would explode like a volcano.

'How would you feel if that happened to your sister Nikil?'

'I'm really sorry, I don't know what came over me.' Tears fell from his eyes as he spoke to dad.

Mum and dad were mad with him and showed no sign of forgiveness. Nikil's dad did all the talking. He told me that I should come home and start all over again.

'Nikil didn't know what he was doing. He was messed up.' He said.

Couldn't he speak for himself? Man, I was furious with him.

'Please forgive him Tina'. Said his dad.

'No, I'm not going back'. I refused

His dad begged me. He said people were talking and he said Nikil had changed. I mean, come off it, did they really think their son had changed? Leopards never change their spots so how was Nikil going to change? Nikil came over and gave me a hug, but I was so angry that I couldn't hug him back. I kept refusing him. Then after an hour they left without me.

You know, we Asian girls are so soft, we kind of think about the whole universe before we think about ourselves. As we're girls, nobody cares one bit about us. We make sure everybody is OK before we even think about ourselves. You know, that's what makes us different, because we think like that. I can't see anyone else being as damn gullible as I was. Dad asked me to give Nikil one more chance. Maybe I was expecting him to say,

'Look, Tina, that guy's not worth it anymore. Forget it'.

But no, he didn't say that. He wanted me to go back and try again. I mean I'd given him three chances, wasn't that enough? Well, anyway, Nikil rang and I went back. Believe me, this was his final chance. If he blew this one then that was it. Although I hated what he had done to me, I still felt so much love for him. He was my first love and maybe even if he didn't feel that much love for me I thought the world of him. I just wanted everything to go back to how it was between us. When he phoned, he seemed he wanted to give it another go.

I was still fuming, but I still loved him. It's strange even after how much he hurt me my heart still reached out towards him. It's easy falling in love with someone but falling out of love isn't that simple. You can't just let the feelings disappear from your heart. It doesn't work like that. I could now understand what Denise went through when Richard broke her heart. It's so hard. It's like an addiction; you cannot live or carry on without that person. Life seems pointless. That's how I felt. I felt life didn't mean a thing after this.

12 I now felt that we needed time away from the family home. We needed space to think and get back on track. So we booked a holiday to Spain. It wasn't a long holiday; just a few days to get us back together, without interference from anyone. I thought this would be a good opportunity to work out our problems.

Then something happened which I never expected. While we talked in the hotel one day Nikil said something, which made me want to die.

'Tina, I don't love you'.

His words went round and round in my head. I stood on the balcony looking directly at him. He was sitting on the bed, looking straight back at me. I didn't know how to handle the situation. I needed to get out, so I ran.

I ran and ran until Nikil caught up with me and grabbed my arm. He apologized but said again that he didn't love me. How dare he tell me that he didn't love me!

I had asked him before we got married and he said nothing. Now he wanted me out of his life. I asked why he had married me in the first place, and do you know what that idiot said?

'I did it to keep my parents happy.'

I really felt like killing the guy. Did he even think that he had now ruined my life? It would be alright for him, he was a guy, but what chance had an Asian girl got of marrying again? Once you're divorced people treat you as if you're diseased. I explained to him that his younger sister, Pooja, would find it hard to find a partner if we separated because of the community gossip. But that idiot couldn't care less. He had said what he had wanted to say, and that was that.

So what did he want me to do then? Pack my bags and go home like I was on a summer holiday or something? Then he mentioned a divorce and I clearly told him how I felt about that. To him this may all have been a joke but I never married him for a laugh. I married him because I loved him and because I wanted to spend my life with him. But then where had all the culture disappeared to all of a sudden? Didn't he believe in anything? It was obvious I didn't mean a thing to him.

'So what do you want me to do Nikil?'

'I don't feel anything for you,' he replied quietly.

'Then why did you marry me?' I shouted, tears fell as I spoke.

'To please my parents.'

'What? You did this to make your parents happy, have you gone mad! I yelled. 'Do you know what you have done, you have ruined my life, have you even thought about it? Did you think I would never find out about you and your girl?'

He stood there listening not saying a single word.

'It's her you love isn't it? That Marie Cooper or whatever her name is. I thought you said she was dead, did she come back again from the dead! This isn't a joke damn you! Oh and what's going to happen to Pooja, can you imagine what she's going to think when she comes back from abroad?'

'She's already got someone.'

'Oh so it's all planned out is it?'

'So what do you want now Nikil?'

'I want a divorce?' He whispered quietly.

'What? You want a divorce!' I could feel myself shaking; the words I never wanted to hear had finally been said.

'There's no point in carrying on like this, I don't love you.'

'You mean you never loved me; you had no intention of loving me did you? Why didn't you think before committing yourself! I don't believe in divorce, I will not divorce you! You hear me, I will not divorce you!'

After coming back home, knowing he didn't love me I still stayed at his place. What did he want me to do? I felt unwanted and sleeping with him was like sleeping with a betrayer. We both slept right on the corner of the bed, our heads in the opposite direction. It was horrible. I couldn't live like this; it was killing me. I had to tell someone what he had said and then, one day, I just blurted it out to my mum and dad. I told them what Nikil had said. You should have seen them; I had never seen my parents so upset.

I wish it hadn't come to this but I really had no choice. I just couldn't continue living a false life. My health was deteriorating, and I didn't know who I was pleasing at the end of the day. My parents decided that after this there was no chance of them sending me back. Dad said he had pulled too many strings. So after that they kept me at home.

My dad spoke to Aunt Simrin's friend who had helped in getting Nikil and I together. They both decided to go over to Nikil's house to discuss the marriage. It was nice to hear that Nikil's parents said that I wasn't to blame for the marriage breakdown. Nikil didn't turn up, as he knew we would question him. What a chicken! Nikil's dad commented that he was a grown man who knew what he was doing that he couldn't keep telling him over and over again. He wasn't a child any more. Nikil's dad showed his concern saying that if we got back together then he didn't know how long it would last again before something else happened. He had a point. As I said earlier, a leopard can't change its spots. Well, that turned out to be another wasted trip because Nikil didn't show up and we couldn't really decide what to do.

A few days later we all went again to discuss the marriage problem and this time Nikil was in the house. He sat upstairs while we discussed the marriage. Nikil's parents said how he had kept them in the dark about the other girl. They said they couldn't see their son changing and that they felt it was better that we went our separate ways. I felt even worse when I saw that they had packed all my clothes and belongings. Then, all of a sudden, Nikil came downstairs and, you know what that idiot said,   'Stop this crying and get your stuff and get out of here. I wish I had never met your family!'

This hurt us very much. I could have slapped him but something inside me didn't let me do anything. My mum and dad were really shocked and saddened at his behaviour. We were so shocked; we all just stood there looking at him. His parents didn't say a word either. There wasn't any point in saying anything now. He had made it clear that there was no chance of us getting back together again.

What more could I do?

'I thought you may have played with my feelings but it won't be long before it comes around to you too. Someone above is watching us even if you didn't believe a damn!' I said bitterly.

It was my worst nightmare. To top it all, I couldn't get him out of my head. I kept thinking to myself that he would phone and say he was sorry but you know that day never came. Instead, he sent me a letter saying he wanted to divorce me. That really hurt me. I couldn't put myself back together again. For such a long time I felt really dirty and unclean knowing he had slept with someone else. I just couldn't help feeling so used.

Top it all, it wasn't easy getting a divorce, it cost me an arm and leg because I was working. He was clever. He had planned this from day one and because he knew he was going to divorce me, he quit his job just so that he could get legal aid. What made it worse was that the idiot lied through his teeth that I didn't cook for him, that I didn't socialize with his family and all that rubbish. His parents did the typical Asian thing and stuck up for their dear son. The community was gossiping that I had a boyfriend not Nikil. The boy can never be at fault can he? It always has to be the girl.

The gossip only stopped after Aunt Anisha told everyone what had happened. He even got away with that rubbish.

The best thing to come out of it was the knowledge that I wasn't wasting my life away with someone who didn't appreciate me. I'm not saying it was easy; of course it was very hard. Just like a typical Asian girl (B.A.G) I started afresh and became more independent. I didn't rely on my parents or family. I decided the ball was now in my court and I was going to play it how I wanted.

Now you're wondering whether an arranged marriage does actually work. Well, after my incident with Nikil I didn't think it did work, but if I'm honest it's Kismet at the end of the day. It could have happened even if I had a love marriage but maybe not in the same way. Maybe I was one of the unlucky ones to see love in such a horrible way. I always thought that when I met my dream guy that he would show me all the love in the world, but how wrong I was. In reality that's not the case.

As for Nikil he hasn't married again yet, in fact he and Marie split up very soon after, and his sister ran off with another guy.

I do have a few tips to share with you should you find yourself in a similar situation to me:

1. Get to know the guy before you marry him; just think it's a lifelong commitment.
2. Marriage isn't a fantasy; it's you who will have to live with the consequences, not the family.
3. Don't get deceived by looks. OK, so looks are

important, but the guy's personality is more so.

4. If you're worried about something, don't be afraid to question him, even if it makes you look stupid.

5. Trust your instincts.

6. Be independent; don't rely on family and friends too much. Make sure you have your say.

7. Remember life is an experience. You're not always going to follow the right path. You may stumble once in a while, like I did but with time, you can fall in love again.

8. And, finally, good luck! I still believe there's someone for everyone. Life is a rollercoaster; you just don't know what's around the corner.

Like a typical B.A.G I didn't sit around feeling sorry for myself, I got up and did something I wanted to do and that was to host my own radio show.

'Hi I'm Tina Sinhasi on Radio BMT and today my topic is 'How do you trust that guy! 'Well after my experience, I find it quite difficult to trust anyone but that doesn't mean to say, that all guys are not trustworthy. Maybe mine was just a one off. Our first caller on the line is Sunita. Hi Sunita, where you calling from?'

'Hi Tina, I'm calling from Liverpool, I'd just like to say that I just love your show. I listen to it every morning. You know, it's nice to have someone you can talk to about Asian problems. I'm going to get married too and, do you know, after listening to your programme, I think I'll be very careful. I'm not going to jump into marriage. I'm going to get to know him, because I find that in Asian marriages we don't seem to get to know the person and that's where it's all going wrong. I think a while ago there were fewer Asians going out but that's all changed which is why we have to be more careful.'

'Well, thank you Sunita for sharing your views. Let me know when your big day is and, if you encounter any problems, then do share them with us.'

As for me, I married again 18 months later. Well I could have stayed single but I didn't want to be alone, sure, I had dreams but I wanted a family too. My Grandmum invited me to India to find a husband but I declined, as I knew it wasn't the way I wanted to meet someone. I became friends with a nice man at work, he was kind and generous and when he asked me out I decided to trust my instincts this time and date him. We went out for a year before we tied the knot. Marriage second time around has been a very different experience; we're very happy together and have two lovely daughters Sneha and Priya. I guess if I hadn't had my bad experience with Nikil then I'd never know the happiness that I have now.

GLOSSARY

Kulfi	Ice Cream
Meri beti!	My daughter
Moto	Fat
Lengha	Asian Skirt
Dupata	Scarf
Hi rabba	Oh my god
Mein mar java!	I'm going to die
Kasam se! Woh shrabi akiya!	Honestly those gorgeous eyes (passionate)
Choli suit	Asian Dress
Suhaag raat	Wedding Night
Masala	Spice
Tina tu mar gayi!	Tina, you're dead!
Jadoo	Magic
Kismet	Destiny